PIRATE SCHOOL
Yo-Ho-Ho!

by Brian James
illustrated by Jennifer Zivoin

Grosset & Dunlap

For Santa, in thanks of all the gifts!—BJ

Merry Christmas to Aunty Paula, Uncle Glen,
Jonathan, and Lauren!— JZ

GROSSET & DUNLAP
Published by the Penguin Group
Penguin Group (USA) Inc., 375 Hudson Street, New York, New York 10014, USA
Penguin Group (Canada), 90 Eglinton Avenue East, Suite 700,
Toronto, Ontario M4P 2Y3, Canada
(a division of Pearson Penguin Canada Inc.)
Penguin Books Ltd., 80 Strand, London WC2R 0RL, England
Penguin Group Ireland, 25 St. Stephen's Green, Dublin 2, Ireland
(a division of Penguin Books Ltd.)
Penguin Group (Australia), 250 Camberwell Road, Camberwell, Victoria 3124, Australia
(a division of Pearson Australia Group Pty. Ltd.)
Penguin Books India Pvt. Ltd., 11 Community Centre,
Panchsheel Park, New Delhi—110 017, India
Penguin Group (NZ), 67 Apollo Drive, Rosedale, North Shore 0632, New Zealand
(a division of Pearson New Zealand Ltd.)
Penguin Books (South Africa) (Pty.) Ltd., 24 Sturdee Avenue,
Rosebank, Johannesburg 2196, South Africa

Penguin Books Ltd., Registered Offices:
80 Strand, London WC2R 0RL, England

Library of Congress Control Number: 2007051076

ISBN 978-0-448-44887-9   10 9 8 7 6 5 4 3 2 1

Chapter 1
Message in a Bottle

"Blimey!" I shouted as I came onto the deck of the *Sea Rat* and saw my best mate Gary leaning over the rail. One slippery step and he'd be shark bait for sure!

I raced over as fast as I could. That's because Gary's not only my best mate, he's also the clumsiest pirate kid who ever sailed the seas.

I grabbed his belt and yanked him away from the railing!

We both stumbled back to safety. I

wiped my forehead and let out a big breath. "That was a close one," I told him.

"Aye," Gary said. Then he reached under his pirate hat and scratched his head. That's what he always did when he was confused. "Arrr, *what* was a close one?" he asked.

"You almost fell overboard, that's what!" I said.

Gary shook his head. "I wasn't falling," he said. "I was just leaning over so I could toss that bottle really far."

"Aye? What bottle?" I scratched my head.

Gary pointed over the side of the ship. I took a peek. There was a bottle floating out to sea. "That's my Christmas list," Gary explained. "I hope Santa gets it in time."

"Great sails!" I shouted. I'd been having so much fun since coming to the *Sea Rat* for Pirate School that I forgot all about Christmas! "When is Christmas?" I asked.

"It's only three days away," Gary told me.

I GULPED!

I hadn't even made my Christmas list yet. So I started pacing the deck and tapping my head. That's how I did all my best thinking.

Just then, Vicky and Aaron came up on deck.

"Ahoy," Vicky shouted. But I didn't shout anything back. I was too busy thinking.

"Arrr! What are you doing?" Aaron asked, pointing at me.

"Pete's trying to come up with his Christmas list," Gary told them.

Vicky wrinkled her nose and gave Aaron a funny look. Then Aaron gave her the same funny look back. That's because they're twins. Twins share the same funny looks.

"Aye?" Vicky asked. "What kind of list is that?"

"Shiver me timbers," I said. "You mean you guys never heard of Christmas?"

They both shook their heads back and forth.

"Is it another one of Rotten Tooth's stinky chores?" Aaron asked.

Rotten Tooth was our teacher at Pirate School and the ship's first mate. He was the meanest pirate on the seas. Plus, he didn't like us one bit. He was always coming up with gruesome new chores for us to do. But even Rotten Tooth couldn't ruin Christmas.

"Arrr, Christmas isn't a chore at all," I said. "It's a holiday!"

"Aye!" Gary said. "On Christmas, Santa Claus gives every kid whatever presents they ask for."

"Aye?" Vicky clapped her hands and smiled really wide. "This Santa guy sounds like a shipshape mate," she said.

"Don't be daft," Aaron said. "Nobody goes around giving kids treasure just because they ask for it. These guys are trying to yank our timbers."

"Arrr! You don't know that," Vicky yelled. Then she squinted her dark eyes into a mean look.

"Arrr! It's a true fact," I told them. "Santa goes all around the world and gives gifts to kids. But only if they're good."

"Hogwash!" Aaron said. "I never got anything!"

Vicky started to giggle. "That's because you're never good," she said. Then we all started to laugh, except Aaron. He folded his arms and huffed.

"Arrr," he grumbled. "You never got a gift, either."

"Maybe Santa didn't give you any gifts because he didn't know what you wanted," I told them. "You should make a list, too."

"Aye!" Vicky agreed.

Aaron frowned. "It still sounds like a trick to me," he said.

That's when Inna came skipping across the deck. She was always the last one ready for school. That's because she's the only pirate kid in the whole wide world who took a bath and brushed her hair every day.

"Ahoy," I said. "We're all making Christmas lists. Do you want to make one?"

Inna shook her head. "No, thanks," she said.

"Aye?" I couldn't believe my ears. If anyone liked presents, it was Inna. "Why not?"

"Because she knows it's a bunch of muck, just like me!" Aaron answered.

Inna put her hands on her hips and huffed. "You're a blunder brain," she told Aaron.

"So you do believe in Christmas?" Vicky asked.

Inna stomped her foot. "Of course I do," she said.

"Aye? Then why don't you want to make a list?" I asked.

"Because I already made one," she said. "I always make my list the first day after Christmas. That way I know Santa will get my list first, and he won't run out of what I want."

"Arrr, that's good thinking," I said.

I was going to do that next year. But first things first—I still didn't know what to ask for this year. I didn't want to ask for just any old present. I wanted the perfect present. It was going to take some tough thinking to figure it out!

Chapter 2
No Such Thing!

"ARRR! Pay attention!" Rotten Tooth growled.

His stinky breath blew right into my face. It made me turn as green as his hair. I had to pinch my nose to keep from getting icky sicky all over the place.

"Line up and stow yer gabbing!" he ordered.

"Aye aye," we mumbled. Then we gave him a pirate salute. That's because he was the boss of us and pirates always salute their bosses, even if they are rotten.

"Ye scurvy barnacles have wasted enough of me time," Rotten Tooth roared. He always thought we were wasting his time. Only this time, it was sort of true. He was trying to teach us how to plot a course at sea, but we were too busy thinking about presents.

"Arrr! Plotting courses is boring!" Aaron grumbled. "Teach us how to swashbuckle and we'll pay attention."

Rotten Tooth squinted his eyes really small. I thought for sure he was going to make Aaron walk the plank! "Mayhap you'd rather scrub dishes in the galley?" he threatened us.

Aaron GULPED.

"Arrr, maybe we should ask Santa for a new teacher," Vicky whispered to me.

Only she didn't whisper it quietly enough.

Rotten Tooth had the best hearing of any pirate on the *Sea Rat*. I didn't even have time to giggle before he snatched us both up by our collars.

We DOUBLE GULPED!

"Are me ears waterlogged or did I hear ye mention Santa?" Rotten Tooth snarled at us.

We nodded our heads up and down.

Then . . . *THUMP*!

Rotten Tooth dropped us to the deck, right on our butts!

"AVAST! Listen up, pollywogs!" he shouted to all of us. "That Santa stuff is a bunch of muck!"

"Gullyfluff!" Inna shouted. She marched right over to Rotten Tooth and tugged on his pointy beard! A lot of the times, Inna was a fraidy pirate, but for some reason she was never afraid to stand up to Ol' Rotten Guts! "Santa is as real as this ship!" she told him.

"Aye," I agreed.

"Yeah, AYE!" Gary and Vicky said.

Even Aaron nodded his head. I'm not sure he really believed. He just didn't want to be on Rotten Tooth's side.

"It's a story for wee babes, not for pirates," Rotten Tooth said. "Ye are wanting to be pirates, right?"

I nodded.

"Arrr, we're not babies!" I said. "We're

already shipshape pirate kids. In fact, Captain Stinky Beard says we're already shipshape pirates, not just kids."

"Right, he did," Rotten Tooth said. "And since ye are pirates, I don't want any more of this Santa talk getting in the way of ye duties, savvy?"

"Aye aye," we mumbled.

Rotten Tooth went back to teaching our lesson. He pinned a map to the mast. There was a dotted line zigzagging across it. He said plotting a course was really about keeping the ship on the dotted line.

I tried my best, but I just couldn't pay attention.

I wasn't the only one, either. My mates were daydreaming, too. If Rotten Tooth took his eyes off the map and saw us, he would blow a gasket for sure!

Just then, Gary raised his hand.

Rotten Tooth hated when we asked

questions. But rules were rules, and the rules said he had to call on anyone who raised his hand. "Arrr, what is it?" he asked.

Gary scratched his head. He fixed his glasses and stared at the map. "Um . . . do you think Santa plots a course to get to all the kids?" he asked. "Because if he plots a course and we keep sailing, he won't be able to find us!"

Rotten Tooth's face turned bright red. I thought I saw steam come out of his ears.

"ARRR! THAT DOES IT!" he roared. He tore down the map and pointed below deck. "I warned ye! Now it's off to the kitchen for ye lot!"

We moaned and groaned. But orders be orders, so we headed off to do our chores. I still didn't know what I wanted for Christmas, but I did know something else. It was NOT going to be easy to get Rotten Tooth into the holiday spirit!

Chapter 3
Setting Sail

"Sink me!" Vicky said as we entered the kitchen. There were stacks of dishes everywhere!

"Aye, this is going to take forever," Gary complained.

Inna glared at him. She got really mad whenever we had to do anything gross and dirty. So she grabbed Gary's hat, pulled it down over his ears, and bopped him on the head. "Arrr, this is all your fault!" she shouted.

"Aye," Aaron said. "All your silly Santa talk got us in trouble."

"Blimey! It's not silly," I said. "It's serious business."

All of my mates gave me a surprised look.

"I've been thinking, and what if Gary's right? What if Santa can't find us? On my old ship, we were always anchored on Christmas."

Inna scrunched up her nose and thought. "Arrr! Me too," she said.

"Aye, me three!" Gary said.

Vicky's eyes went really wide, and she turned to Aaron. "Maybe we were always at sea and that's why we never got presents?"

Aaron crossed his arms and lifted his chin up in the air. "Maybe," he mumbled. I could tell he still didn't believe, but he had to admit it was possible.

"If that's true, then Christmas is ruined!" Inna grumbled.

"Pirates never give up," I said, shaking my head. "That's part of the pirate code and good pirates always follow the code. All we need is a plan."

"Aye, that's a good plan," Gary said.

"Aye," Vicky agreed.

"Aye!" Inna said. "I'm not letting some pirate kid get my gifts just because Santa thinks we're lost at sea."

Then we all turned to Aaron.

"Arrr, I still say it's a bunch of hogwash," he growled. "But if there's a chance to get some treasure, then I'll help."

"That's the spirit, mateys!" I said.

We all put our hands into a circle and gave our pirate cheer.

"SWASHBUCKLING, SAILING, FINDING TREASURE, TOO.

BECOMING PIRATES IS WHAT WE WANT TO DO!"

Then we tried to come up with a plan.

"I know," Vicky said. "If Santa can't find us, maybe we can find him."

"Aye," Gary said. "I heard a Christmas story that said Santa lives at the North Pole."

"Aye, that's it!" Inna said. "All we have to do is get the *Sea Rat* sailing due north."

Aaron rolled his eyes. "How are we supposed to do that, blubber brain?"

"Arrr! Maybe we could fill the sails with all the hot air in your guts, Captain Big Mouth!" Vicky shouted at him.

I didn't like it when my mates fought.

I stepped between them and held up my hands.

"Hold your sea horses," I said. "I have an idea. What if we plotted a course like Rotten Tooth showed us? Then we could distract the pirate on steering duty and switch the maps. Nobody would even know."

"Arrr, but won't Captain Stinky Beard get mad when he finds out?" Gary asked.

Inna jumped up and clapped her hands.

"Not if we throw a surprise holiday party for the whole crew," she said. "No one can get mad if there's a party. That's a true fact."

"Aye, that's good thinking," I said.

"I'll plan the party," Inna said.

"Me and Aaron will figure out a good distraction," Vicky said.

"Aye aye!" I nodded. Usually they weren't a very good team. But when it came to being sneaky, they were shipshape. "I'll write a letter to Santa and let him know we're coming. Plus, I'll add our wish lists, so you'll need to tell me what you want to ask for."

"That's easy! I want a sword," Aaron said.

Vicky squinted at him. "I thought you didn't believe in Santa?"

"I don't," Aaron said. "But just in case he is real, I'm not going to miss out."

"If he's getting a sword, then I want one, too," Vicky said. "I'll need to protect the rest of us when he starts swinging it around like a monkey."

"Aye," I giggled. "And I'm going to ask Santa for a treasure map."

"Arrr, why not just ask for treasure?" Vicky asked.

"Because," I said, "it'll be more fun to find it together."

"Aye," she agreed.

Then it was time to get to work.

Inna headed back to our bunks to make decorations. Aaron and Vicky snuck back above deck to scout around. I sat down at the dining table and started writing my letter.

Before I finished one word, Gary tapped me on the shoulder.

"Um, Pete?" he asked. "Aren't we forgetting something?"

Gary pointed to the gruesome dishes covered with gruel.

"AYE!" I said.

Gary and I were going to have to scrub the dishes by ourselves. My letter would have to wait until we were done. Saving Christmas was going to be one dirty job, but it sure was worth it!

Chapter 4
Top Sneaky Mission

"Arrr, the coast is clear," I whispered, poking my head out of our quarters and into the empty hallway. We'd waited for most of the crew to start snoring before we put our plan into action.

"If Rotten Face catches us sneaking about, we'll be in big trouble!" Gary said.

"Arrr! Don't be a scallywag," Aaron said. "This is going to be easy breezy."

"Arrr, I hope you're right," I said. Our plan *was* pretty tricky. Everything needed to go shipshape to pull it off.

I slipped open the door and made sure it didn't creak. Then I snuck into the hallway. Inna, Vicky, and Aaron snuck behind me.

Gary snuck after them.

Then . . . *WHAM*!

Gary wasn't very good at sneaking, and the door slammed shut behind him.

"Arrr! Way to go, blunder head!" Inna whisper-shouted.

"Sorry," Gary mumbled.

"C'mon, let's go, mateys," I said and tiptoed down the hall. We could hear the other pirates snoring in their quarters as we snuck past. Then we raced up the galley stairs as fast and as quietly as we could.

"Looks like we're in luck, mates," Vicky

said when we didn't spot any pirates on deck. The pirate on duty was Long Legs Billy, the ship's navigator. He was busy minding the wheel.

"Arrr! The first thing we have to do is distract him," I told my mates.

"Righto! I got it all figured out!" Aaron said. "Me and Gary will sneak around to the other side of the ship. You guys go over there and talk to him. When I shout 'Man overboard,' you guys switch the maps."

"Arrr, why do you get to do the fun part?" Vicky complained.

"Because!" Aaron said. "It was my idea."

Vicky rolled her eyes. "Arrr, I guess you do have the biggest mouth," she said.

"Aye," Inna giggled.

Aaron grumbled. But there wasn't any time to waste on arguing, so I stepped between him and Vicky before they could start.

"Let's go, buckoes," I said.

Gary raised his hand. "Um, Pete?" he asked. "Does that mean I have to go overboard? Because I don't want to go overboard."

"Quit blubbering," Aaron said. "It's only for pretend."

"Arrr, okay," Gary said with a smile. "I like pretending."

"Then it's all settled," I said.

"Aye aye!" Aaron and Gary said and gave me a pirate salute. Then they snuck away and Vicky led me and Inna over to where Long Legs Billy was piloting the ship.

"Ahoy, lil' shipmates," Billy said when he saw us coming. "What brings ye out here so late?"

Vicky had an answer all planned out. "Arrr, Rotten Tooth's been teaching us to plot courses," she said. "We just wanted to see how you followed one."

Long Legs Billy smiled. "I'll be happy to show ye," he said.

As he was pointing out different stars and explaining how to steer the ship in a straight line, Inna was busy drawing a dotted line on a new map. The new line would take the *Sea Rat* straight to the North Pole.

She was making a few last marks when all

of the sudden, we heard a shout.

"MAN OVERBOARD!"

Long Legs Billy turned around. "Arrr, what's that?" he asked.

Vicky shrugged her shoulders.

"Maybe we should take a look," I said.

"Aye," Billy said.

Vicky raced around the corner. Billy stepped away from the wheel to follow her.

"Pssst, hurry!" I whispered to Inna.

"Aye," she said. Then she snatched away the map Long Legs was following and put our map in its place. It was just in time, too—Billy was about to sound the alarm bell!

Vicky came racing back around and stopped him. "Arrr, it's only my blunder-headed brother," she said. "It was a false alarm."

Long Legs Billy wiped his forehead. "Arrr, that be a relief," he said.

It was time for the final part of our plan. I inched closer to Billy and peered at the map. Then I scratched my head and pretended to be confused.

"Arrr, Billy? Are you sure we're on course?" I asked.

"Aye! Sure I'm sure," he said.

"But look at the stars," Inna said, pointing up at the sky. "Now look at the map. If Rotten Tooth taught us right, I'd say we're off course."

Billy looked up and down.

"Leaping dolphins!" he said. "Ye pups

are right, we *are* off course!"

I looked at my mates. We all had to cover our mouths to keep from giggling.

Then Billy hollered out orders to two pirates who were snoozing on deck. "Man the ropes," he shouted. "Turn the ship about. Full sails ahead!"

The *Sea Rat* started to turn and picked up speed.

"We'd better go back to our quarters," I said.

"Aye, it's getting late," Inna said with a yawn.

"Aye," Billy said. "Thanks for helping out, mates."

"No problem," Vicky said.

We met up with Aaron and Gary. "No one spied us," they reported.

"Shipshape," I said. "Now let's double time back to our quarters before we get caught."

"Aye aye!" Vicky said.

We raced back to our quarters.

"Let's get some shut-eye," I said.

Vicky and Aaron jumped onto their bunks. Inna closed the pink curtain around her bed. Gary lay down on his bunk, and I climbed onto my bed above his.

"Sleep tight. Don't let the ship bugs bite," I said.

Inna huffed.

I forgot she didn't like the bug part. I had too much on my mind to remember. That's because there was one last order of business before I could go to sleep.

"The list," I mumbled to myself.

I reached under my pillow and took out the letter for Santa. I put it there to keep it safe. I looked it over one last time and then shoved it into a bottle. Then I opened the porthole window and tossed it out. Now nothing could stop Christmas from coming!

Chapter 5
Right On Course!

"Shiver me timbers!" I said as soon as I woke up. That's because my timbers were really shivering. Plus, my teeth were chattering.

"Aye, you can say that again," Vicky said.

I looked over at her bunk, but I couldn't see her. That's because she was completely wrapped up under her blanket.

Then I heard a noise coming from Gary's bunk.

"Arrr . . . arrr . . . arrr-choo!"

I looked over the side of my bed. It was Gary. He sneezed so hard, he fell out of his bunk!

"I think the cold got inside me when I was sleeping," he said.

"Aye," I said and wrapped a blanket around my shoulders. "I think we're sailing toward the North Pole. Our plan must have worked."

"Aye?" Aaron poked his head out from under his blanket. "It was one stinky plan, then! I think my feet have turned into ice cubes!"

"Arrr, I think your brain's an ice cube," Vicky said.

"At least I have a brain," he said.

"Arrr! That's not the Christmas spirit," I told my mates. "Plus, Santa knows when you're fighting. He won't give presents to kids who fight."

"Says who?" Aaron asked.

"Arrr! It's true," Gary said. He pulled out his book of pirate tales and turned to the story about Santa. Then he pointed to a picture of Santa holding two lists. "There's a good list and a bad list, and Santa checks it twice. Kids on the bad list don't get presents—they get seaweed slop!"

As soon as he finished, we all heard jingling and jangling coming from Inna's bed. It sounded like treasure rattling. Only it was less rattly and more jingly. We didn't know what was making that noise, but it sure sounded happy.

"Good morning!" Inna shouted.

She opened the pink curtain that hung over her bed and looked around. When she waved, there was more jingling. That's when we saw her bracelet. It was made of bells.

"Arrr! What is that?" I asked.

"It's part of my Christmas outfit," she

said. "So is this coat and this hat." She picked up a heavy red coat and a red stocking cap and put them on. They both had fuzzy white collars and looked very, very warm.

"Arrr! That's just like what Santa wears," Gary said.

"Aye!" Inna smiled. "And guess what?" Inna handed a hat to each of us. "I made each of you your own hat, that's what!"

I put mine on. It wasn't very piratey, but it sure was warm.

"Arrr, thanks mate," I said. "This is a shipshape present!"

"Aye," Gary and Vicky agreed.

"Arrr! I'm not putting that on," Aaron complained.

"Quit bellyaching!" Vicky hollered at him. "You said you were cold, so put the hat on already! We have to get on deck for school."

Aaron made a grumpy face, but he put the hat on anyway.

Then we all raced out of our room and up the stairs.

It was even colder outside than it was in our quarters! It was so cold, Gary's glasses fogged up. He almost stumbled overboard.

I took them off and wiped them.

"Arrr! Thanks, Pete," he said.

"Sure! That's what best mates are for," I told him.

Then we looked all around. Rotten Tooth was nowhere to be seen. But we did spot Captain Stinky Beard. He was scratching his beard and staring at a map in his hand.

"Ahoy, Cap'n," I said and gave him a salute.

"Ahoy, me little shipmates," Captain Stinky Beard said to all of us. "Have ye noticed that it's colder this morning than usual?" he asked.

"AYE!" we all shouted.

"Arrr, me too!" he said. He looked at

the map some more, and I noticed it was the map with Inna's course plotted on it. "Something's fishy," the captain said.

"Aye, Cap'n!" Rotten Tooth growled as he came toward us. "Mayhap I can take a look at that," he said, pointing to the map. Captain Stinky Beard handed it to him. After all, Rotten Tooth was the best course plotter on the *Sea Rat*.

I crossed my fingers really tightly.

I was scared he would figure out our trick.

"ARRR! Something be fishy all right," Rotten Tooth mumbled as he studied the map.

I looked at my mates, and they looked at me. Then we all gulped. We thought we were going to be shark bait for sure!

"Aye?" the captain asked.

"Aye, but it's not the map," Rotten Tooth said. "According to this here map, we're right on course. The only thing fishy is the weather."

"Aye! A storm must be a-brewing," Inna suggested.

"Aye! A really big storm with lots of cold stuff," Aaron added.

Rotten Tooth glared at them. "Stow it," he said.

"Arrr! The wee ones may be right," Captain Stinky Beard said. "We better get the ship ready for a storm just in case."

"Aye aye!" Rotten Tooth said.

I wiped my forehead and let out a big breath. "That was the closest one in the whole history of close ones," I whispered to Vicky.

"Aye," she whispered back.

The captain headed back to the main cabin. Rotten Tooth started to batten down the hatches.

I raised my hand. "Arrr, what do you

want us to do?" I asked.

"I want ye pollywogs to STAY OUT OF ME WAY!" Rotten Tooth roared. "School's canceled for today. Make yerselves scarce belowdecks, savvy?"

"Aye aye!" we shouted.

It was the best news we'd heard in days. We still had gifts and decorations to make for the surprise holiday party.

"ARRR! AND DON'T BE SO MERRY ABOUT IT, EITHER! THAT'S AN ORDER!" Rotten Tooth shouted.

"Aye aye," we mumbled. Then we pretended to mope all the way back to the galley stairs. But as soon as that scrooge was out of sight, we went right back to clapping and skipping and being very merry!

Chapter 6
Spreading Cheer!

"Sink me! I never knew making cards was so much work," I said. My fingers were aching from cutting and folding paper.

"We have to keep working," Inna told me. "We need enough for everyone on the crew."

I looked at the pile of cards in front of me.

"Arrr! Isn't that enough?" I asked.

I had already cut and folded about a gazillion cards. I wasn't sure exactly how many. Pirates aren't very good at counting. But I was sure it was close to one gazillion.

Inna stared at the pile. Then she put her finger on her chin. That meant she was thinking. "Hmm," she thought. "Maybe make six more."

"Aye aye," I moaned and started cutting and folding again.

Inna went back to work, too. She was writing *Merry Christmas* on every card. Then she handed them to Gary. His job was to draw a star on them with paste and sprinkle over it with glitter.

"Avast! I think we need more paste," Gary said.

"Arrr, that's because you have more of it on your shirt than on the cards!" Inna said.

"Arrr! It's not my fault," he said. "It keeps sticking to me."

Inna crossed her arms.

"That's its job!" she hollered. Then she got up and went over to the closet. She took out another jar of paste and brought it to Gary. "Here!" she said and dropped it on the table.

The dust from the jar blew right into Gary's face. He was still a little bit sneezy because of the frosty air, and this made him a lot of a bit sneezy.

"Arrr . . . arrr . . . arrr-choo!" he sneezed.

Glitter went flying everywhere!

"Um . . . I think we need more glitter, too," Gary said.

"YOU BLUNDER HEAD!" Inna shouted. "I don't care if I don't get any presents, I'm still going to bop you on the head!"

She reached over and pulled Gary's cap over his ears. She was just about to bop him over the head when she had to stop and cover her nose.

"Grimy guts!" I said, covering my nose, too. "What's that stink?"

Inna's face turned green. "I don't know, but I think I might be icky sicky."

Just then, Vicky and Aaron came barging in. They were carrying huge plates piled high with gruesome grub. "Ahoy, mates!" they shouted.

"Ahoy," I said. Then I pointed to the plate and stuck out my tongue. "Arrr, what is *that*?"

"Blimey!" Vicky said. "These are the presents we made for everyone!"

"Aye?" I asked.

"Aye!" Aaron said. "Sea slug cookies! They're the yummiest!"

"If you say so," I said.

"Aye, but there's only enough for the party,"

Vicky said. "So promise not to sneak any!"

"WE PROMISE!" I said.

Inna and Gary nodded their heads up and down. There was no way they were going to sneak any of those cookies, either!

"We're almost done with the cards," Inna told them. "After that, we need to make ornaments for the tree."

"Arrr! We don't have a tree," Vicky said.

Inna smiled really wide. "I know that," she said. "That's why we have to pretend the main mast is a tree!"

"That's good thinking," I told her.

"Aye," Vicky said. "This is going to be the best surprise Christmas party I've ever been to."

"Arrr, it's the only one you've ever been to!" Aaron said.

Vicky glared at him.

"So? It's still going to be the best!" she hollered.

"Aye!" I agreed.

We all put our hands together in a circle and got ready to say our pirate cheer. Only this time, we changed the words:

"GETTING, MAKING, AND GIVING GIFTS, TOO.

SAVING CHRISTMAS IS WHAT WE WANT TO DO!"

Then we all started cutting, pasting, and glittering decorations. We were so busy that we hardly noticed how cold it was getting on the ship. By the time we finished, it was so cold that each of us could see our breath, even below deck!

Chapter 7
Lookout!

"Please! Please!" I begged.

"Pretty please with seaweed on top!"
Vicky added.

Rotten Tooth rubbed the two ends of his
pointy green beard and glared at us. "Arrr!
Why would ye be wanting to volunteer for
night lookout duty?" he asked.

I reached under my Christmas cap and
scratched my head. I was trying to think of
an answer. "I know," I said. "Inna thinks
there might be a mouse in our quarters,
and she's a scallywag about mice."

I glanced over at Inna. I was worried she
might be mad. But then I remembered that
Inna was a clever pirate, and she knew it
was part of my plan.

"Aye," Inna said. "Maybe it will go away by morning."

The real reason we wanted to be lookouts was so we could watch for Santa. Plus, we had to put up the holiday decorations while the crew was sleeping. If we told Rotten Tooth the truth, he'd never let us stay up.

"Arrr," Rotten Tooth mumbled and rubbed his beard some more. "Maybe freezing out here for a night will teach ye not to be so afraid of mice," he said. "So as yer teacher, I'm ordering you to be on lookout duty!"

"Aye aye!" we cheered.

Rotten Tooth gave us a suspicious look.

We all covered our mouths and remembered not to act merry. It worked. Rotten Tooth gave us one last grumble and then headed below deck.

"Arrr! Let's get started," I said once the deck was clear.

We decorated the main mast to make it look like a Christmas tree. Then we put all the cards and presents around it.

"Perfect!" Inna declared.

"Aye," I agreed. "Now let's get up to the crow's nest and wait for Santa!"

"Aye!" Aaron agreed. "Last one there is fish guts!"

We all raced up the rigging and piled into the crow's nest. Up there, we could usually see everything. But this time it was different. When we looked out to sea, we couldn't see anything!

"Pete? I think my glasses are foggy again," Gary said.

"I think my eyes are foggy," Aaron said.

"Arrr! I think your brain is foggy!" Vicky said.

"Stop calling my brain names!" Aaron hollered.

I held up my hands and made them both shush. "Avast," I said. "Something's wrong with the sky."

All my friends looked up to see that I was right. Little pieces of the clouds were falling onto our heads.

Inna screamed and covered her eyes.

"ARRR! The sky is breaking apart!" she yelled.

We all ducked down and covered our heads.

Only Gary didn't duck down at all. He was laughing.

"What's so funny?" Inna sneered.

"It's only snow," Gary said. We all made *ooohhhs* and *aaahhhs*. We'd heard about snow, but none of us had ever seen real live snow before. "It always snows at the North Pole," Gary told us. "It must mean we're getting close."

"Arrr, I knew that!" Aaron said.

"Arrr, you were hiding, too, Captain Big Mouth!" Vicky reminded him.

"I was just trying to make you guys feel safe," he said.

Vicky rolled her eyes and tried to ignore him.

Then it started to snow harder. Soon, the whole sky was full of snow. "How are we going to look for Santa now?" Inna asked. "I can't see anything!"

Then, all of a sudden, there was a huge *CRASH*! The *Sea Rat* stopped dead in its tracks. We were almost thrown right out of the crow's nest!

"ARRR! WHAT WAS THAT?" Vicky yelled.

"I don't know," I said. "But we better go check it out."

We each grabbed onto a rope and swung down to the main deck. Then we raced to the front of the ship and peeked over the railing.

"Great sails!" I shouted.

I couldn't believe my eyes! The ship was stuck right in the middle of an island made of ice! The sea was frozen solid.

"Arrr! Let's try to break it," Gary said.

"Aye!" Aaron agreed. He picked up an oar and threw it at the ice like a spear. But the oar bounced right off and slid away into the blizzard.

"We need a plan," I said.

"Aye!" my mates agreed.

Only we didn't have time to think of a plan because the rest of the crew was already making their way onto the deck.

We GULPED!

"Arr, I think we're in really big trouble this time!" Gary said.

I nodded.

"Aye!" I said. "Even if the ship isn't stuck forever, Captain Stinky Beard's probably going to kick us out of Pirate School when he finds out it's all our fault."

Chapter 8
Caught Red-Hatted!

Captain Stinky Beard marched to the front of the ship. My mates and I hid behind some barrels and watched as he peered over the railing.

"Arrr! He looks pretty steamed," I whispered to my mates.

"Great slimy pigfeathers!" the captain shouted when he saw the ship stuck in the ice. "How could this happen?"

My eyes opened extra wide.

I'd never heard the captain sound so angry. Most of the time, he was the nicest captain on the seas. But the other pirates on the ship had told us stories about when Captain Stinky Beard got angry. They said he could be even fiercer than Rotten Tooth.

"Arrr! Who be on lookout duty?" he roared to the crew. They were all gathered around him. Their timbers were shaking and shivering and not just because it was cold. Someone was going to walk the plank because of this!

"Pssst," Aaron whispered. "This is a pretty big blunder. Maybe we should hide somewhere far away?"

"Aye," we agreed. Even Vicky wasn't going to argue with that plan.

We'd just started to sneak away when . . . *WHOOSH*!

Inna and I were lifted right into the air.

I peeked at Inna, but she had covered her eyes with her hands. So I peered over my shoulder instead. A rotten green smile stared back at me.

"Arrr, Cap'n! Here be the culprits!" Rotten Tooth hollered. Then he scooped up Aaron, Vicky, and Gary in his arms, too, and carried us over to the captain.

Then . . . *THUMP*!

He dropped us down on the deck!

"This here mangy lot were on lookout duty," he said.

Captain Stinky Beard squinted and glared at us. "Arrr, is this true?" he asked.

"Aye, Cap'n," we said.

"Aye, but it wasn't our fault," Vicky said. "We couldn't see the ice because of the snow."

"Aye! Plus, my glasses were foggy," Gary said.

"Aye! My eyes were foggy, too," Aaron said.

"Stow it!" Rotten Tooth growled. Then he faced the captain. "There be more to it,

Cap'n!" he said. "I've been watching these sprogs and they've been acting fishier and fishier the closer it gets to Christmas. They've been wearing those silly caps. And I found decorations and presents by the main mast. Now the deck is covered in snow, and the ship is stuck in ice! I'd say we're somewhere near the North Pole and that these pollywogs are to blame!"

We DOUBLE GULPED!

The captain scratched his beard. "Arrr, that's impossible," he mumbled. "I've checked the course every hour. This can't be true, can it?" he asked us.

We all looked at one another. None of us wanted to get caught, but I knew we had to tell the truth.

I stood up straight and raised my hand. "Cap'n?" I said. "Rotten Tooth is right. We changed the course because we wanted to see Santa."

The whole crew made *ooohhhs* and *aaahhhs*. It was mutiny to change a ship's course behind the captain's back!

"Arrr, this is very serious," Captain Stinky Beard said.

I hung my head. "Aye," I mumbled. "But we didn't mean for the ship to get stuck."

"Aye," Inna said. "And we planned a party and presents for the whole entire crew. It was supposed to be a fun surprise."

"ARRR! Yer the ones in for a surprise!" Rotten Tooth said. "I say we strand them here on the ice! That be fit punishment for mutineers!"

Then he scooped us all up again and carried us to the railing.

"Put them down!" the captain ordered. "I think they've learned their lesson. And since we're stuck here, we might as well go ahead with that party."

"Aye?" we asked.

"AYE!" he said and smiled really wide. "Ye went through all this trouble. After all, it *is* Christmas!"

"AYE!" the whole crew cheered.

"Yippy skippy!" we shouted.

"So, where be those presents?" the

captain asked us.

"Arrr, dead ahead!" I said. Then we led the entire crew over to the main mast and started the holiday party.

Chapter 9
'Tis the Season for Giving!

"See! I told you they were yummy!" Vicky said when she saw the crew munching down on the sea slug cookies.

"Arrr, I guess you're right," I admitted. I still didn't know how anyone could eat those yucky snacks. I had to pinch my nose anytime I caught a whiff.

"Ahem," Inna interrupted. "Don't you think it's time to give out the presents?"

"Aye!" I said.

We had made special presents for our favorite members of the crew.

"Let's give Clegg his present first," Aaron suggested.

"Aye!" we agreed.

Clegg was the oldest, nicest pirate on

the *Sea Rat*. Plus, he was our friend. He always told us the best stories.

We found Clegg sitting near the fire that Rotten Tooth had made on deck to keep everyone warm. "Ahoy, me little shipmates," he said. "This be a fine party."

"Thanks," I said. "But it's not over."

"Aye?" he said.

"Aye!" Inna said. "We all made you a special gift!"

Vicky was hiding the present behind her back. It was a homemade book. "Surprise!" she hollered and handed it to Clegg.

"We each made a drawing of our favorite stories that you've told us," Gary explained.

"And we made them into a book all by ourselves!" Inna said.

Clegg smiled really wide and flipped through book. Then he pointed to his eye patch and said, "I might not be able to see so well, but me one good eye thinks these look shipshape!"

"Arrr, but mine's the best," Aaron bragged. Since it was Christmas Eve, we let it slide.

Clegg thanked us again, and then it was time for us to give Captain Stinky Beard his present. It was a necklace made of shark teeth!

"Blow me down!" Captain Stinky Beard said. "This is a real nice gift."

"Aye!" Vicky said. "Every captain should have one."

Inna leaned close to the captain. "Arrr, I thought we should paint it pink because a necklace is supposed to be pretty. But they wouldn't listen to me."

Captain Stinky Beard smiled and patted Inna's head. "Arrr, that's okay," he told her. "It's the thought that counts."

We had one more gift to give out.

I looked all around the deck until I spotted Rotten Tooth sitting all by himself. "He doesn't look very jolly," I told my mates.

"Arrr, maybe his gift will cheer him up," Vicky said.

We raced up behind him and tapped him on the shoulder. "ARRR! What do ye pups want?" he grumbled.

"We want to give you a Christmas gift," I said.

"Aye?" Rotten Tooth asked.

"AYE!" we shouted.

I handed him his gift. It was a Christmas cap

57

just like ours, only a lot bigger. Plus, we wrote something special with glitter. "It says 'World's Best Pirate Teacher!'" I told him.

Rotten Tooth looked really surprised. His eyes got all red, and I was worried he didn't like the gift. "Arrr, I don't know that I be deserving this," he mumbled.

"Of course you do!" Vicky said.

"Ye really think I'm the best pirate teacher?" he asked.

"Aye!" Inna agreed. "If you didn't teach us how to plot a course, we wouldn't even be having Christmas!"

It was the truth. Even if Rotten Tooth was the grumpiest teacher ever, he was still the best. Then we all leaned over and gave him a great big hug.

"Arrr," he said. "This be the best present I ever got." Then he put the cap on and joined the rest of the crew. We sang sea carols for hours and hours!

Finally, everyone was getting sleepy. It was time for bed. But before we went back to our quarters, the captain stopped us. "Arrr, you never said what ye wished for," he said.

"Me and Vicky wished for swords so we could swashbuckle," Aaron said.

"I wished for a brand-new dress," Inna said. "But not just any dress, one with lots of ribbons and bows. Plus matching ribbons and bows for my hair."

"Arrr, and I wished for a new book of pirate tales," Gary said.

Captain Stinky Beard smiled and said those were all good things to wish for. Then he looked at me. "What about you, me lil' buccaneer? What do you want for Christmas?"

"I wished for a treasure map so me and my mates could go on an adventure," I said. "But you know what? I don't even want that anymore, that's what!"

"Why not?" the captain asked.

I lowered my head. "Because all I want for Christmas now is for the *Sea Rat* to get unstuck, since it was all our fault."

My mates thought about that and nodded their heads.

"Aye," they all mumbled.

Captain Stinky Beard told us that was a noble thing to say, but it didn't make us feel much better. "Arrr, it'll be dark for a few more hours. Perhaps Santa will still bring you what you want."

"Aye?" we asked.

"Aye!" he said. "Now off to bed before he catches you awake."

"Aye aye!" we said. Our spirits were cheered up. If the captain said there was still a chance we'd each get our wish, then there must be. Captains know everything!

Chapter 10
Merry Christmas!

The next morning, I was sound asleep when all of the sudden my eyes popped open. That's because I heard a really loud *BANG*!

"Arrr! Santa?" I shouted.

I sat up in my bunk and looked around.

"Arrr, it's only me," Gary said. "Sorry, I fell out of my bunk again."

"Arrr, that's okay," I said. Then I noticed something fishy out the porthole window. "Blimey! We're sailing again." I couldn't believe my eyes! There was no ice anywhere to be seen.

Aaron sat up in his bunk and looked out the window, too. "See, I told you we wouldn't be stuck forever," he said.

Vicky was about to argue with him, but then she noticed something else fishy. "AVAST!" she shouted. "GIFTS!"

When I looked over the side of my bunk, I double couldn't believe my eyes! All the presents we asked for were there in our quarters.

Two wooden swords for Aaron and Vicky!

A fancy dress and ribbons for Inna!

A treasure map for me!

And the biggest, fattest book of pirate tales for Gary!

We all rushed for our presents and scooped them up. "I knew Santa would come," Inna said as she tried on her dress.

"Aye," Gary said, flipping through his book.

"Arrr, and YOU didn't believe," Vicky teased Aaron.

"Arrr, I was only yanking your timbers.

I knew it was true all along," Aaron joked. He picked up his sword and he and Vicky started jumping all around the room, pretending to swashbuckle.

Then there was a knock on the door. It was the captain and Rotten Tooth. They looked super-surprised when they saw our presents. "Arrr, looks like Santa came after all," the captain said.

"Aye!" I shouted. "I got both presents. The ship is unstuck, and I got this shipshape treasure map. From the picture, it looks like a lot of treasure!"

"Do you think it was really Santa?"

Gary asked them.

The captain looked at Rotten Tooth, and Rotten Tooth looked at the captain. They both shrugged and smiled.

"Hard to say," Rotten Tooth said. "But I did find this on deck this morning." He pulled something out of his pocket. It was a cap like ours, only different.

"Great sails!" I said. "That must be Santa's cap!"

"Aye," my friends said.

"It just might be," Captain Stinky Beard said.

Inna rushed over and grabbed it. "We'll send it back to him," she said. "Tomorrow we're making our lists for next year. We'll stuff this in the bottle, too. That way he gets it in time for next year."

"Aye aye!" we said.

Then we all went back to looking at our gifts. Next Christmas was still a whole year away. We wanted to enjoy this Christmas as long as we could. After all, we all agreed this was the best pirate Christmas ever!